WITHDRAWN

THE MYSTERY AT THE CALGARY STAMPEDE

created by
GERTRUDE CHANDLER WARNER

Illustrated by Anthony VanArsdale

Albert Whitman & Company
Chicago, Illinois

Library of Congress Cataloging-in-Publication
data is on file with the publisher.

Published in 2015 by Albert Whitman & Company

ISBN 978-0-8075-2840-2 (hardcover)
ISBN 978-0-8075-2841-9 (paperback)

Printed in the United States of America
10 9 8 7 6 5 4 3 2 1 LB 20 19 18 17 16 15

Illustrated by Anthony VanArsdale

For more information about Albert Whitman & Company,
visit our web site at www.albertwhitman.com.

Contents

THE MYSTERY AT THE CALGARY STAMPEDE

CHAPTER 1

Cow Town

In the airplane seat ahead of Benny and Henry, a man put on a white cowboy hat.

"Does that mean we're about to land?" six-year-old Benny asked his big brother.

"We still don't know where we're going!" said Jessie, age twelve. She sat across the aisle from her brothers, and next to her was her younger sister, Violet.

"It's a mystery," said Violet. She couldn't believe they were about to land and their grandfather still hadn't told them where they were going.

The plane began to descend and Violet reached for her grandfather's hand. "I'm not afraid," she whispered.

"I know," Grandfather said. He gave her hand a soft squeeze.

Violet felt good with Grandfather beside her. She could remember a time when she and her brothers and sister found an abandoned boxcar in the woods and made a home for themselves there. That was before they'd met Grandfather. But now Grandfather took care of them, and they cared for him too—Henry in his fourteen-year-old, big brother way, and Benny, always quick to make everyone laugh. Now the boxcar had a home in their backyard.

Violet squeezed Grandfather's hand right back, and he smiled at her.

"Ready for adventure?" he asked.

"Always," she said.

"So," said Henry as the plane taxied toward the airport, "where are we?"

Grandfather chuckled. "I'm going to let you guess." He led the way through the airport and onto a bus.

Half an hour later, Benny was kneeling on his seat, looking out the window. “All the windows of shops and restaurants and offices in this city are painted with cows and horses and cowboy hats and boots.” He pointed to a revolving door in a tall building. “Look at that! It’s painted like old-time Western saloon doors!”

Grandfather pulled on the cord to let the driver know they were getting off the bus.

Violet pointed to another painted window. “Look—it says, ‘Welcome to Cow Town.’ Is there really a city with that name?”

Henry shook his head. “I think we’re in the city of Calgary. Grandfather, you told us about it when you were telling us about your friend Judy. It’s also called Cow Town, you said. And my guess is that it’s Stampede time. Right?”

Grandfather smiled wide. “You’re right, Henry! Cow Town Calgary, it is.”

Benny was frowning. “What’s a stampede?” he asked. “Isn’t that when everybody rushes around and somebody gets knocked over?”

“Like this?” asked Jessie. She jogged in

STAMPEDE!

circles around Benny. Henry and Violet danced around too. Benny squealed, and Jessie lifted him up and gave him a squiggly, tickling hug.

"I think stampede has more to do with horses," said Henry. "You know, broncos bucking and roping calves and riding bulls like cowboys."

"That's called a rodeo," added Jessie.

"Right!" said Henry.

Grandfather spoke up. "The rodeo is one part of the Stampede. The Stampede includes all sorts of events, from art exhibits to dog shows. We're going to have a great time!"

They'd come to a building with a sign that read *Glenbow Museum*. A woman was standing in front. She had a huge smile on her face and bright red hair that sat in a pile atop her head.

"Our Calgary Stampede is called the Greatest Outdoor Show on Earth," she said in a deep, rich voice. She must have overheard them. She put out her hand. "I'm your grandfather's friend, Judy Simon!"

She shook each of the Aldens' hands and chuckled. "I thought it was about time your grandfather brought you to our province of Alberta."

"In Canada a province is like a state," Jessie explained to her siblings.

"I'm so excited you're all finally here," Judy said. "Especially for Stampede time! Every July we open our city to the world for ten days. It's a giant party! We have cowboys from all over North America. We have chuckwagon races and young people exhibiting animals they've raised. We have a marvelous midway fair with rides and food—"

She noticed Benny's eyes widen. "Did I mention *food*?" Judy laughed. "You'll find some very strange foods at the Stampede."

Benny opened his mouth to ask her about the strange food, but she was already leading them into the museum.

"I want to show you something on the second floor," Judy said, heading to a wide staircase. "And I want you to meet my niece, Daisy, who is joining us. I have a surprise for her!"

On the second floor were two large signs with arrows pointing in opposite directions.

One read *Picturing the Northwest*, and the other read *Our Historic Stampede*.

"Let's go that way," said Benny, pointing to the second sign, and the others followed him.

Judy chuckled. "I like how you leap right in."

Jessie stopped in front of a wall lined with posters. "The Stampede's been around a long time. Look, there's a poster for every year."

"*This* poster is for the Stampede in 1912!" pointed out Violet.

"Look at this poster!" said Jessie. "It's from 2012 and says it's the hundredth anniversary of the Stampede!"

Grandfather stopped in front of a huge painting.

"Well, well," he said to Judy. "It's so lifelike that if you weren't standing in front of us, I'd guess that was really *you*." The painting was a portrait of Judy standing in front of a concert marquee that read: *Judy Simon: Live at the Grand Ole Opry*.

Jessie remembered Grandfather telling them about how Judy traveled all over the world. She realized his friend must be a famous country music singer.

Judy laughed. "It *is* very odd to see myself like that!"

Benny was staring hard at the portrait. "What is that pin you're wearing in the painting?"

"You have sharp eyes," said Judy. "That's my Young Canadian pin. That was given to me for being part of the singing and dancing troupe that performs every evening at the Stampede Grandstand Show. I was a Young Canadian for five years so they gave me a special pin with my name engraved on it!"

"Five years! That must have been a lot of work," said Jessie.

"It was," Judy said. "And it was how I got my start as a singer." She lowered her voice to a stage whisper. "The pin is the surprise I told you about. I'm going to give it to my niece Daisy. She's meeting us here to see my portrait for the first time. She had to miss the unveiling of the portrait because she was at rehearsal. But she doesn't know that I want to celebrate *her* too!

"Daisy is now a Young Canadian," she explained. "I have a feeling that this is the beginning of her own singing career. I'm so proud of her. Her first time performing on the Calgary stage is tomorrow night!"

Violet gave a squeak of excitement, and she turned to Grandfather. "Do we get to see the show?" she asked.

Before Grandfather could answer, Judy said, "Of course you do."

Just then a girl about Henry's age with bright red hair and a wide smile that matched Judy's ran up to give Judy a hug. "Auntie Judy!" she exclaimed.

Jessie knew this had to be Daisy.

Daisy saw the portrait of her aunt. "Oh my," she said. "It's beautiful!" She stepped back. "Look at that! The artist even put your pin on it."

"The pin you've wanted since you were a little girl," said Judy. "Now here you are, a Young Canadian yourself and ready for your first opening show!"

Suddenly Daisy looked anxious, but her aunt put an arm around her. "You'll be just fine. Look," Judy said, pointing to the Aldens. "My good friend is visiting with his grandchildren. They'll be staying with me."

She introduced Daisy to the children, one by one. The Aldens learned that Daisy lived just down the street from her aunt.

"I hope you like Calgary," Daisy told them.

Benny beamed. "We will!" he said. "We can't wait to see your show!"

"Oh, it's not *my* show," said Daisy, her voice uneasy.

"You know," said her aunt, "I was going to wait until after dinner tonight but I think I'll give you my pin right here and now!"

Daisy was surprised. "Really?"

"I want you to have it," Judy told her. "You can wear it tomorrow night. I love the thought of my pin on the Stampede stage once again." She pulled a small velvet box from her pocket, took out the pin, and pinned it onto her niece's collar.

The Aldens clapped and Benny cheered.

Daisy ran her fingers across the shiny pin. "I've been so nervous about being onstage. But with this, I know I'm ready to perform. My feet will fly in all the right places when I dance, and I'll hit all the right notes when I sing."

"You'd do all that even without my pin," said Judy. "I didn't mean for you to think that you *need* the pin."

Daisy threw her arms around her aunt and gave her another hug.

Everyone started talking at once with excitement. Daisy was like a bright light in the middle of them, and Benny couldn't stop staring at her. She looked as if she was going to spring into dance or burst into song.

As they were all talking, something caught Henry's eye. An older man was standing by Judy's portrait. Henry thought that the man had been there for a while and that maybe he'd seen Judy give the pin to Daisy. The man looked about Grandfather's age, with a heavy, graying beard. He was shorter than Grandfather, with a wiry build. Henry couldn't see his eyes because the man was wearing a very large cowboy hat.

The man stepped up to speak to Henry. "That's a special pin," he said in a low voice. "That piece would be a nice addition to the museum!" He explained, "I'm an amateur collector of Stampede memorabilia myself."

All the conversations stopped just then as Daisy noticed the man.

The man smiled and motioned to the painting. "Congratulations, ma'am," he said to Judy, "on your many accomplishments. And you, young girl"—he turned to Daisy—"are very lucky."

Daisy didn't seem to know what to say. Judy reached out to shake the man's hand, but he'd already turned away. "It's a beautiful pin," he said gazing at the portrait. "Not too many of them around. Hope you don't mind…" he said and took an old-fashioned camera from the big leather bag hanging from his shoulder and snapped a picture of the portrait.

Before anyone else could say anything, he walked away.

Benny whispered, "That cowboy hat is so big it makes him look like a cartoon." He stopped. "I didn't mean to sound rude," he added, "but it did."

Jessie smiled. "I know you didn't mean to sound rude, Benny. It is a *huge* hat.

"I thought *he* was rather rude," said Judy.

"It was odd how he looked at the painting,"

said Henry. "He was so curious about the pin and even took a picture, but he didn't introduce himself or shake your hand."

Judy shrugged and waved her hand dismissively. "We have something *very important* to do now," she said. "We need to celebrate! I have a special Welcome-to-Calgary dinner planned for all of us."

Benny was pleased with this plan. "Dinner *is* very important," he said. "Let's go!"

CHAPTER 2

Parade Day

The next morning, Judy—who had told the Aldens to call her "Aunt Judy"—got up early to pack food and blankets. She was ready to take the children to the parade while Grandfather went to a business meeting.

Benny peeked in one of the food containers and was excited to see chicken wings left over from the celebration dinner the night before.

"I have a collection of cowboy hats," Aunt Judy told the Aldens. "You can each choose one to wear." She looked at Violet. "I have a purple one for you. It's my favorite, but I'll share it while you're here."

When the Aldens had picked out their cowboy hats, they all headed out in Aunt Judy's minivan, picking up Daisy along the way. Aunt Judy and Daisy lived in the city, and downtown was only fifteen minutes away.

"Let's find a spot on the corner of Fifth Street and Ninth Avenue," Aunt Judy said once she found a parking space. "I want to show you something."

The streets were closed to traffic there, and every corner of the intersection was filled with people waiting for the parade. Aunt Judy and Daisy chose a place to set out their blankets on the edge of the curb.

"What's all that?" asked Jessie, pointing to a spot in the middle of the intersection where the pavement was marked in large numbered squares.

Daisy laughed. "*That* is horse poop bingo."

"*What?*" Benny's mouth gaped open. The pavement *did* look like a giant bingo card, but without the B-I-N-G-O letters. They walked over to the squares for a better look.

"I don't see any horse poop," Benny said.

"Not yet," said Aunt Judy. "That will come. Soon."

The Aldens spotted a man with a bucket. On the bucket was a sign: *Horse Poop Bingo*. Coins rattled in the bucket.

"Over here!" Aunt Judy called out to him.

She rummaged in her bag, and pulled out five big coins. "These are nicknamed 'toonies,'" she told the Aldens. "Canadian *two*-nie dollar coins! Each one is worth two dollars. Get it? I'll give one to each of you and Daisy. You choose a number in a square where you think some horse poop might end up...and if a horse poops in that square, you can win some money. The rest of the money goes to a charity."

The man with the coin bucket gave Jessie a piece of chalk to share and write their names in the squares of their choice.

"I'm twelve, so I'll pick the square with that number," said Jessie. Henry, Violet, and Daisy each chose a square too.

Benny chose the square he was standing on.

Then the Aldens went back to their blankets to wait for the parade to begin.

Benny stood on the curb and peered down the street.

"I see bagpipes," Benny called out. After another few moments, he added, "And a band!"

Soon they could all see the Calgary Stampede Show Band marching down the street toward them.

Violet shivered in excitement. Behind the band came a mint-green convertible with the parade marshal sitting in back. Now the parade had truly begun! The crowd cheered and waved.

Henry looked up and noticed people standing in the windows of all the downtown office buildings; they were even on the rooftops. The entire city and all its visitors seemed to be celebrating together.

Next came a group riding beautiful, chestnut-colored horses. "Maybe one will poop in my square," said Benny. He looked for his square, but couldn't see it with all the people on the street.

Another marching band led by baton twirlers went by, followed by Ukrainian dancers, Greek dancers, and Hawaiian dancers. A little girl doing an Irish dance moved her feet faster than anything Benny had ever seen. He almost forgot all about the horse poop until a horse went by and did just that, though not on one of the Aldens' squares. The crowd cheered as the horse went past. Benny noticed that they didn't seem to care whose square was lucky. Everyone was just happy the poop was on a square.

A line of covered wagons went by. Daisy recognized someone in one of the wagons. "Look," she said to the Aldens, "there's another Young Canadian." She waved, and a boy with black curly hair waved back. "His name is Clay."

Beside Clay was a little girl with black braids. She wore a long, checkered pioneer skirt and a bonnet. She waved too.

"Is that his little sister?" asked Violet.

"She is. She's like his little shadow," said Daisy. The girl waved too.

The parade continued with more people riding by on horseback. Even the mayor rode a horse! He was followed by the Royal

Canadian Mounted Police in fancy red jackets clip-clopping past on their horses.

Violet watched the Calgary police officers as they strolled up and down along the curbs. They wore black cowboy hats with red bands on them. She'd never seen a police cowboy hat and thought they looked quite adventurous. She also noticed all the different colored cowboy hats in the crowd. She was hoping to see purple cowboy boots but didn't spot any.

One of the parade floats had a sign that read *Cow Town Amateur Archives* in fancy old-fashioned-looking letters. On the float were a bookcase full of old books and boxes. The boxes were labeled in big letters: *Old Photos and Maps* read one. Others said *Letters and Postcards*, and *Memorabilia.* A man in a very big cowboy hat was kneeling over one of the open boxes, looking as if he was busy sorting through papers.

Daisy pointed to the back of the float, which was decorated with dark green fabric that looked like waves, and a low wall made up of sandbags "That part of the float represents the flood," she told the Aldens. "Calgary had a terrible flood a few years ago. So many places were under water, and a lot of historical items were ruined. Some things were rescued before the flood reached them, and some were damaged and needed to be restored. I think that's what this group does—finds and preserves and stores old stuff so that we can study it later."

"What are *archives*?" asked Violet.

"Archives are very old things—historical records like diaries and letters or even the old Stampede posters you saw at the museum," said Aunt Judy.

Henry nudged Jessie and nodded toward the float and the man with the large hat. "I think that's the man we saw at the museum yesterday!"

Jessie squinted. "He does have a beard... and that big hat sure looks familiar!"

The man looked up from the boxes to wave to the parade spectators, and Henry was sure he *was* the man from the museum!

When the last float had gone by, the Aldens, Aunt Judy, and Daisy joined the river of parade-goers heading toward the fair. The streets were packed and hot, but the crowd seemed friendly as if everyone knew one another.

Benny grabbed Daisy's hand, and she smiled at him. "Welcome to the Calgary Stampede," she said. "The celebration has now officially begun!"

Aunt Judy, Daisy, and the Aldens headed to Stampede Park, where the grandstand, rodeo arena, and many of the other Stampede attractions were taking place. Daisy had rehearsal with the Young Canadians before the show that night, so Judy dropped her off at the south gate to the park.

"We'll be back in time for the show," Aunt Judy told Daisy. "Break a leg!" The Aldens knew that meant "good luck."

"I have my pin," said Daisy. "That's all the luck I need." She touched the pin on her collar. "I really do feel lucky."

Aunt Judy watched her niece disappear through the gate. "She doesn't really need the pin for luck, you know," she told the children. "She has a full chuckwagon's worth of talent."

"I can't wait to see her tonight!" Jessie said.

"I have a busy afternoon planned for us," said Aunt Judy. "First, we'll take a drive along the Bow River."

"What about dinner?" asked Benny.

Aunt Judy chuckled. "I thought we could go back to the food section of the midway, and fill up on deep-fried pickled beans!"

Benny looked uncertain. He liked to think he could try any sort of food, but deep-fried pickled beans just did not sound good!

"I told you we had some very strange food here," Aunt Judy said. "How about we have homemade macaroni and cheese with bacon at my place instead?"

Benny nodded and grinned.

***

After an afternoon drive and dinner at Aunt Judy's, it was time to go back to Stampede Park. Aunt Judy and the Aldens made their way to the grandstand.

Jessie noticed the grandstand was starting to fill with spectators as she and the others followed Aunt Judy to the Young Canadians' dressing rooms.

"This is one of the biggest mobile stages in

the world," Aunt Judy explained. "During the day, it's parked just outside the rodeo arena. The rodeo events and the chuckwagon races are in the arena throughout the day, and then at night the entire stage is pulled by a huge tractor right into the middle of the arena."

Henry and his siblings thought a stage that could be pulled by a tractor sounded amazing. "I can't wait to see it," he said.

They had reached the dressing room entrance. "Good evening, Ms. Simon," the security guard said as he waved Aunt Judy and the Aldens through. It seemed to Jessie that Aunt Judy could go wherever she wanted.

The dressing room was loud and bright. A group of girls was warming up with singing exercises, and their warbly bird sounds made Benny and Violet giggle. Another group of teenagers were on their toes dancing in circles.

"Look," said Jessie, pointing toward the mirrors. "There's Daisy's friend Clay from the parade."

Clay was sitting in front of a mirror, putting gel in his hair, which was thick and kept falling across his face. The gel didn't seem to be helping, and he got up to look for something.

His little sister was sitting next to him. "I told you to let Mom cut it," she said to Clay.

"Daisy was right," Henry told Jessie. "His little sister does seem to follow him around all the time." They watched as the little girl, who looked to be about five, stood up and followed her big brother as he looked around the dressing room.

Clay came to a stop in front of them. "You haven't seen a cowboy hat around here, have you by any chance? I've got to cover this up." He pushed his fingers through his messy hair.

"I've seen a lot of cowboy hats." Jessie laughed. After all, in this city, cowboy hats were everywhere!

A look came over Clay's face. Jessie thought maybe he'd suddenly remembered where his hat was. He ran out of the room, bumping into people in his rush. His little sister stayed behind, looking confused.

"I wonder what that was about," Violet remarked.

Clay came running back a few moments later, his hat on his head. "Whoa! Sorry," he said to the Aldens. "I didn't mean to be rude. I just remembered where I left my hat." He grinned and shook their hands. "I'm Clay."

"And I'm Little Clay," his little sister said.

"Do you have your own name?" asked Jessie, smiling at the little girl.

"Yes," she said. "But I like to be Little Clay. I'm going to be a Young Canadian too someday."

At that moment a woman called to the little girl from the doorway. "Honey!" she said. "We need to go."

"Oh, that's my mom. Got to go!" Little Clay danced over to her mom and they left.

Jessie turned back to Clay. She was going to ask him where he'd found his hat.

But suddenly they heard a cry from the lockers by the doorway. Everyone turned to look.

"My pin!" shrieked Daisy. "Has anyone seen my aunt's pin? It's gone!"

Chapter 3

A Pin for Good Luck

Jessie could tell that everyone in the dressing room knew what Daisy was talking about. She must have shown them all the pin.

"Don't panic," called out Aunt Judy. But Daisy was already in tears.

Some of the other Young Canadians tried to reassure her.

"I'm sure it will turn up," one boy said.

"It has to be somewhere around here," said a girl in a bright blue sundress. She looked close to tears herself.

A few more Young Canadians searched the dressing tables, looked under costumes, and checked the floor.

"Where did you last see it?" Henry asked.

Daisy wiped her eyes. "It was in my…"

Suddenly a voice boomed over the PA system. "Young Canadians! Places in three minutes!"

"Oh no," whispered Daisy. "How can I go onstage without my pin?"

Violet grabbed her hand and held it tight. "You can do it," she said. "Your aunt said you have a whole chuckwagon full of talent. And I believe her. Don't you believe your aunt?"

Aunt Judy spoke up. "You have the talent, Daisy! You know it!"

Daisy looked at Aunt Judy and then at Violet, and after a moment she nodded. She sniffed and shook her head. "I need to get ready to go on," she said. "I'll look later, when the show is over."

"We'll find your pin for you," said Jessie.

"We're good at finding things," added Benny.

Daisy dried her eyes and put on the last touches to her makeup. Aunt Judy looked on sadly. Jessie wondered if losing the pin bothered her. Was she worried for Daisy?

***

The Aldens and Aunt Judy watched the show from the wings of the stage. It began with a burst of music as performers in country costumes, glittering with sequins and stars and bright fringe, filled the stage.

"How many Young Canadians *are* there?" Jessie whispered. Onstage, rows of teenagers were performing a musical routine with sticks and wagon wheels. They circled the wheels in the air over their heads as though they were feather light. It seemed magical. Benny's eyes were huge, and Jessie had a feeling he was going to try something with their old hula-hoop when they got back home.

The next act was a dance number, with the Young Canadians tap-dancing in a circle formation. Daisy danced in the middle by herself as other dancers stepped back. Violet remembered how anxious Daisy had been about the pin and wondered if she would be all right.

Daisy held up her microphone, and Jessie

could see that her face had gone pale. She touched the collar of her shirt—the place where the pin should be—and looked over at Aunt Judy. Then she began to sing.

Her first note was too soft as if she was scared. Henry could see Aunt Judy bite her lip and whisper something under her breath. But the audience burst into excited applause. Daisy became even paler. She sang a song about wagon wheels moving through long prairie grass. "*We keep rolling, looking for home...*" But after a moment, her voice faltered again.

"Oh no," said Aunt Judy, and she reached for Violet's and Benny's hands.

From where they were standing, the Aldens could see Daisy trembling. But just then Clay and another girl in the troupe stepped forward and stood beside Daisy. Clay sang the melody with Daisy and the other girl sang harmony, and together they sounded good. Daisy smiled at Clay and then at the girl, and she looked so relieved.

"They saved the day," Aunt Judy whispered. "The show must always go on!"

The show did go on. Even after Daisy's stumble, the show was amazing. Jessie shook off her worries and enjoyed every minute. She hoped Daisy could do the same.

When the Young Canadians finished their performance, a fireworks show began in the night sky over the grandstand.

Suddenly Henry had an idea. The Young Canadians were still onstage throughout the fireworks show. That meant the dressing room was still empty! He realized it would be a good time to search for Daisy's pin. He tugged on Jessie's sleeve and told her his plan.

A few minutes later, the two of them were pulling open drawers and looking under chairs in the empty dressing room.

Henry was peering into cabinet when he heard a squeak from behind a closet door nearby. He pulled it open, and out popped one of the teens he had seen in the dressing room before the show—the girl in the bright blue sundress. She had a flashlight in her hand.

"What are you doing here?" asked Henry. "I remember you. You were here before."

"I work here," she said, turning a deep shade of red. "I'm Marian."

Jessie abandoned her side of the room and joined them. "I'm Jessie and this is my brother, Henry. We're looking for the pin that went missing. Maybe you've seen it."

"No, I don't think so," said Marian quickly, looking flustered. Then she pulled herself together. "I *was* here earlier." She stood straighter. "I hope you don't think that means *I* took it!" She waved the flashlight under Henry's nose. "I've been looking for it myself."

Jessie remembered seeing Marian close to tears before the show. But she waited for Marian to explain herself further.

"Look, I work with the Young Canadians," Marian said. "I help with wardrobe and props. You don't really think I took it, do you?"

"Nobody seems to know what happened to it," Henry said.

"Well, *I* didn't take it." Marian's voice grew firmer as she spoke.

A shadow moved across the doorway just then. A man walked in—the man with the beard and the huge cowboy hat.

"Poppa!" said Marian, and she ran across the room to hug him.

Jessie and Henry looked at each other. *Poppa?* They'd seen this man at the museum and on the parade float—and now he was related to Marian?

Marian turned to the Aldens. "This is my grandfather," she said.

"We've met," Henry said to the man, "at the Glenbow Museum. Though you didn't tell us your name."

Marian's grandfather peered at them

from under the hat. "I'm Darryl Sutton. I remember seeing you. You're friends of Judy Simon."

"Yes, we are," Jessie spoke up. "We're looking for..."

Marian interrupted. "Poppa, Daisy Simon's pin has gone missing!"

"Really." Mr. Sutton frowned slightly. "What could possibly have happened to it?" He pushed his hat back on his head and peered around the room. "That pin would be so valuable in the museum collection," he said. "I was hoping that young Daisy would give some thought to donating it. Maybe she'll do that when it turns up." He fiddled with a buckle on the big leather bag over his shoulder, undoing it and doing it up again.

Henry and Jessie could hear voices from outside and the bustling noise of people coming down the hallway. They knew the show must have ended, which meant the opportunity to look around the empty dressing room was gone. The Young Canadians streamed in and filled every corner of the dressing room. Violet and Benny arrived with Aunt Judy.

Daisy was one of the last performers to come in. "Oh," she said when she saw the Aldens. "Have you been looking for my pin? Have you found it? I really do need that pin for luck!"

She looked close to tears again, and Jessie hated to tell her that they hadn't found the pin yet.

"Where could it have gone? It was right here in my locker." Daisy pulled open the door to her locker to show them. "What am I going to do without it? How am I going to perform tomorrow night? Did you see what happened onstage tonight?"

Aunt Judy spoke up. "Yes, I heard a lovely trio! And that was just tonight. Tomorrow night you'll be fine."

"You sound so sure of that," said Daisy.

Violet was looking around the lockers carefully. Then she surveyed the whole dressing room too. "Who can come in to this room?" she asked. "All the Young Canadians, and who else?"

"Some of us have visitors—family members, mostly." Daisy said. "Really, a lot of people have been through here. Crew people, electricians, newspaper and TV reporters." Her voice grew discouraged. "Maybe it's just…lost. I hate to think that someone took it!"

"Should we call the police?" asked Henry.

"I don't think we need to do that yet," said Aunt Judy briskly. "I think it will turn up. I have a better idea! Let's go home and have some cheesecake to celebrate a wonderful performance tonight!"

"How can you think of *cheesecake* now?" Daisy asked.

"I can always think of cheesecake," said Aunt Judy.

"Me too," chimed in Benny.

Aunt Judy laughed and reached for his hand, and they headed out the door. Daisy followed behind them, her head down. Violet hurried after her, and reached for her hand too.

"Maybe cheesecake will help give us some ideas for solving this mystery," Jessie said to her brother as they followed the others.

"I hope so," said Henry.

Chapter 4

A Cow in My Soup

Grandfather was waiting for the children when they returned to Aunt Judy's. They all sat around the large dining table while Grandfather cut slices of cheesecake.

As Henry served the slices, Jessie looked around Aunt Judy's house. There was a vase of bright summer flowers in the middle of the table that made Jessie think about how Aunt Judy made everything a celebration, whether it was her niece's accomplishment, the Aldens coming to town, or even horse-poop bingo.

Everything felt like an adventure. Jessie wished the Young Canadians show could feel like that for Daisy too.

Then Jessie noticed a large framed photograph on the dining room wall. It seemed to be of a lake—but a familiar-looking building was right in the middle of the water. Jessie realized it was the grandstand at Stampede Park, and the photo must have been taken during the Calgary Flood. A second photo hung on the wall nearby, showing the entrance gate to Stampede Park with trees and people and sunshine all around—just as the Aldens had seen it.

Aunt Judy noticed Jessie looking at the photos. "I put those pictures there to remind me of what people can do when they have to," she said. She pointed to the photograph of the flood. "Rain means so many different things here in the prairies. Sometimes it means we have enough moisture for crops, and rain is a good thing. But sometimes, we get too much and too quickly. That's what happened a few years ago. It rained and then it rained some more, a record-breaking amount. The Bow River and the Elbow River ran high and washed out the bridges and walks along the riverbanks. Stampede Park was filled with water just two weeks before the Stampede began."

"It looks like a lake in the photo," said Jessie.

"What did everyone do?" Benny asked.

"People here in Calgary did what they had to do to keep the Stampede going. We all rallied together and helped clean up just in time. That meant mopping up a lot of mud!"

"Look," said Daisy, and she pulled out a dog-eared magazine from under the vase of bright flowers to show the Aldens. "Here are more pictures. There's even one of Aunt Judy helping, covered in mud and cleaning somebody's flooded house."

"Wow," Violet murmured as she and her siblings looked through the magazine photographs showing flooded houses and roadways and Stampede Park. It was amazing to think the place they had visited today had been covered in deep water.

"Here's a picture of some old musical instruments that were rescued." Henry pointed to one of the pages. "And some old books and photos too. It's good that people save these things from being destroyed. That's what Marian's grandfather, Mr. Sutton, does, right?"

"We should ask him about that," said Daisy. "I thought he was just a strange old man at the museum."

"Speaking of the museum," Violet said, "there's a lot of old stuff about the Stampede there. All those posters and souvenirs. Where did they all come from?"

"Many people donate their old historical things to the museum. They want to share them with the world and make sure they're taken care of. Museums know how to preserve special items."

At those words, an unhappy look passed over Daisy's face.

"What's wrong?" asked Benny, peering at her.

Daisy gave a rueful smile. "Well, when Aunt Judy gave me the pin, I thought about donating it to the museum one day. If only I'd done it right away, the pin wouldn't be missing. The museum would have kept it safe for other people to enjoy." She looked miserable. "But I also wanted to wear the pin myself. I needed it." She shook her head. "What am I going to do tomorrow?"

Aunt Judy changed the subject. What are we *all* going to do tomorrow?" She looked at Benny. "I have an idea," she said. "Why don't we go to the mini tractor pull? I have a feeling you—Benny, especially—will like it."

"I think that's a great idea," said Grandfather. "I'll be busy tomorrow, but I'll join you for the Grandstand Show tomorrow night."

Daisy looked miserable at the mention of the show but the children gave a cheer. "Grandfather, wait until you see Daisy tap-dance," said Jessie. "She's amazing."

Daisy was embarrassed by the praise, but Aunt Judy spoke up. "Daisy has spent hours and hours dancing and singing and learning music. She homeschooled this past year to make time for it all. I'm very proud of her." She gave her niece a hug.

"But I had stage fright tonight," said Daisy.

"It happens," said Aunt Judy. "Do you really think I've never had stage fright? Trust me, wearing a pin won't make a difference."

Daisy didn't look so sure.

As the Aldens helped wash up, Aunt Judy started to sing a funny song about a cow in her soup as they worked. Once they learned the song they all joined in. It felt good to sing. Maybe, Violet thought, the people who cleaned up after the flood sang while they worked.

***

The Aldens shared a great big room to sleep, with bunk beds built into the walls. They liked that they could all be together and talk after lights out.

Violet and Benny were getting sleepy when Jessie spoke up. "You don't think..." she began but then hesitated.

"What?" asked Violet.

"I'm not sure I should even say what I'm thinking," Jessie went on. "But do you think that maybe Aunt Judy took the pin? Just to prove to Daisy that all her practicing would pay off?"

"Oh," said Benny, suddenly wide awake.

Violet cleared her throat. "Aunt Judy kept changing the subject when Daisy talked about the pin. She also said not to bother calling the police yet. And I heard her say that she was sure the pin will turn up when Daisy told everyone it was missing. It seemed like a strange thing for Aunt Judy to say. How could she know for sure?"

"Maybe she just wanted to say something that would make everybody calm down," Benny said.

Jessie nodded. "You are so wise, Benny. That might be exactly right. What do you think, Henry?" she asked.

Her older brother thought for a long minute. "I think that you're right that Aunt Judy really wants Daisy to know she can perform without a good luck charm…but I don't think she'd put Daisy through all this worrying."

"That doesn't seem like something she'd do," said Benny.

"She's too kind for that," added Violet.

Jessie let out a breath of air. "I guess you're right," she said.

The children thought about who else could have taken the pin.

"What about Marian?" asked Jessie. "Her face was so red when we talked to her."

"There's something she's not telling us," said Henry.

"And there's something strange about that big old bag her grandfather—her poppa—carries."

The others agreed.

From outside the open window came a gust of cool air. The children snuggled deeper under the fluffy blankets that Aunt

Judy had set out for them, and one by one they drifted asleep.

Chapter 5

Tractor Pull

The next morning, as the Aldens and Aunt Judy set off in the minivan for Stampede Park, the sky was blue and cloudless. The children could see the dark shapes of the Rocky Mountains to the west, but the sky seemed to go on forever.

Daisy was very quiet when they picked her up at her house.

As they drove through the neighborhoods, the Aldens noticed all the front yards were full of people. They saw tables and chairs set up on one street, and they could smell maple syrup and bacon through the open minivan windows.

"There are lots of pancake breakfasts this week," Aunt Judy said. "It's Calgary tradition for churches and community centers to host pancake breakfasts during the Stampede. There are also lots of block parties."

Violet saw a yard sale sign. "I like yard sales," she said. "I like to find books for my library at home. I never know what I'm going to find at a sale." She wished she could say something that would cheer up Daisy and take her mind off the lost pin.

Aunt Judy seemed to notice Daisy's mood too. "You know," she began, "when I was young I lost something very special to me. I never found it. It bothered me for a long time, longer than it should have. I tried to distract myself by thinking about other things…"

"Like cheesecake?" asked Daisy.

Aunt Judy smiled. "Like cheesecake. Or like Violet's yard sales. Or by remembering to enjoy the day. I wish I could make you forget the missing pin."

The Aldens looked at one another. They knew that Aunt Judy couldn't have taken the pin.

Soon they were outside the main gate of Stampede Park.

"I have rehearsal," said Daisy, as she stepped out of the minivan. "But I'll meet you all for lunch."

"Will we have strange food?" asked Benny.

"How about a bison smokie?" asked Daisy.

"That doesn't sound strange, just different...and good!" said Benny.

Daisy waved and headed through the gate into the fairgrounds.

Aunt Judy handed Henry a map to Stampede Park. "Your grandfather thought you would enjoy having some time on your own today. You can explore the park and go on some rides on the midway."

"What's the midway?" asked Benny.

"At a fair, that's the area where the food stands and rides are located." Aunt Judy smiled. "My favorite was always the Skyride, with the gondolas that glide right over the grounds and you can watch people as you swing through the air. I used to call it the 'Spyride' when I was young."

"I like that name," said Violet. "The Spyride!"

Aunt Judy waved good-bye as the Aldens climbed out of the minivan. "You have fun on the rides. Don't forget to check out the mini tractor pull. Your grandfather and I will meet you for dinner before the Grandstand Show."

"Okay," Henry said as he studied the map. "Let's find the tractor pull. It looks like it's in this direction." He led the way and the others followed after him.

Violet looked up over their heads. "I want to go on the Spyride before we head home," she said.

"Tractor pull first," said Benny. "Spyride later!"

The tractor pull was next to a huge painted sign on the side of a trailer. *Kid Versus Machine*, the sign read.

A man standing next to the sign waved them over. "It's the kids' pedal tractor pull!" he called out. He was wearing the skinniest jeans Benny had ever seen, the biggest, shiniest belt buckle and a cowboy hat of course. "My name's Allan, and this is my assistant, Skippy, and we're going to see to it that you have the tractor pull best time ever!"

Benny looked at the tractors. They were miniature tractors with bike pedals instead of an engine. Benny really wanted to give one a try.

"Pick me!" he asked the man. "Pick me!" He couldn't wait.

The man grinned. "Step right up, young man, step right up. I'll bet you had something like a sugar sandwich for breakfast, and you're ready to race!"

Benny laughed.

"I want to race too!" came a squeaky voice that the Aldens had heard before. It came from Clay's little sister.

Violet couldn't help but stare at Little Clay's cowboy boots. They were purple!

Little Clay smiled shyly at her. "I saw you watching the parade. I liked your purple cowboy hat."

Just then Skippy, Allan's assistant, motioned

to Benny. "You're on tractor number two in lane two."

Benny looked over to the track. At the end of both lanes was a bright yellow ribbon that declared *Finish*. Skippy had lined up the two tractors, and a bigger boy was waiting in the first lane. Hitched to the tractors were little carts carrying big metal weights.

"Those are heavy," said Skippy. "You're going to pull the weights to the end of your lane all the way to the finish line."

"The trick is *to not stop pedaling*," Allan told Benny. "Once you stop, starting to pedal again will be almost impossible." He raised his voice so that all the folks in the audience could hear. "We're going to cheer really loudly so these boys pedal as hard as they can!"

The crowd cheered. Almost everyone let out a "Yee-haw!"

Violet saw Little Clay cross her arms tightly as if to protect herself from the noise.

Benny climbed onto his tractor, and when Allan shouted "*Go!*" he pushed at the pedals. Getting the pedals going took a lot of effort, and the bigger boy was already almost halfway down his lane. But Benny was off, pushing the pedals as hard as he could. The other boy seemed to be slowing.

"Keep going!" shouted Benny. "We can do it!"

The boy looked at him in surprise and paused. When he tried to get the tractor started again, it was too late. Benny could see that Allan was right: *if you stopped, you couldn't start again!* Benny took a deep breath and pushed one foot down, then the other, harder and harder. It felt as if the weights were getting heavier, but he focused on the pedals until he reached the yellow ribbon.

"You did it, Benny!" Henry came over to high-five him. Jessie and Violet clapped their hands in the air.

Little Clay and another girl were up next.

"Let's have a hand for"—Allan bent down to hear Little Clay whisper her name to him—"Little Clay!" he called out. He shook his head. "Is that your stage name?" he asked jokingly.

A big smile came over Little Clay's face. "Yes, sir. That's my stage name!"

He announced the other girl, and she and Little Clay got on their tractors. Allan called out "*Go!*" and off they went.

As the crowd cheered, a frightened look came over Little Clay's face. She turned to look at all the people Jessie thought the little girl might cry. Little Clay stopped pedaling, and the other contestant pulled ahead, but she didn't quite reach the yellow ribbon when she couldn't pedal any farther.

Big Clay stepped out of the crowd. He went over to his little sister and picked her up.

The Aldens could hear her from where they stood. "All the people scared me," she said with her face tucked into his shoulder.

"Poor Little Clay," Jessie said to her brothers and sister. "I think the crowd was too much for her."

"It's funny though," said Violet. "When she was on the covered wagon in the parade, the crowd there didn't seem to bother her."

"But she had Big Clay beside her," said Jessie.

"Give a hand for Miss Purple Boots," Allan called out to the audience, "Also known as Little Clay! She's done good...Yee-haw!"

Everyone echoed "yee-haw" and clapped for Little Clay. She looked up, gave a small smile, and seemed a bit cheerier. But Jessie could understand why a small girl—even one who wanted to be a Young Canadian—could feel a bit lost and frightened.

Just then Violet nudged her. "Look," Violet whispered. She pointed to her own collar and nodded her head in Big Clay's direction.

Jessie took a closer look at Big Clay just as he and his little sister were walking off. There was something shiny on his collar!

"Did you see that?" Violet whispered after

Big and Little Clay had gone.

"There's *something* on Big Clay's collar," said Jessie. "And it sure looks like Aunt Judy's pin!"

Chapter 6

By the River

The Aldens waited to meet Daisy for lunch at the bison-smokie stand.

"I've never had bison," said Benny. "A smokie's like a hotdog, right?"

"A *super* hotdog," said Henry. "It's huge and it has deluxe toppings like onions and sauerkraut and different relishes."

Jessie was thinking. "We'll have to ask Daisy if she saw Clay wearing the pin this morning."

"I'm positive it's the same pin," said Violet.

"But if he took it I don't know why he'd wear it for everyone to see."

"I don't like to think that one Young Canadian would take something from another," said Jessie. "Let's ask Daisy if she knows anything about it."

Benny saw Daisy walking toward the stand. "There she is. That means we can eat."

The others laughed. They each ordered a bison smokie. Benny and Henry heaped sauerkraut on their smokies, along with some weird-smelling mustard that looked like mud.

"This is the best," Benny said. The others nodded, mouths too full to speak.

Violet finished chewing first. "We saw Little Clay at the tractor pull this morning," she told Daisy. "Big Clay was there."

"He said he saw you there," replied Daisy. "It's weird that he happened to find a pin just like mine, isn't it?"

"Is that what he told you?" asked Jessie.

"Yes. He found it at a yard sale a few weeks ago, but he's been letting Little Clay wear it. Then he heard me say that wearing the pin would bring good luck to the performance, and he wants to try it tonight. Especially after—you know—what happened to me last night. So Little Clay gave it back to him.

"I think Marian was a little jealous," Daisy continued. "She told me at rehearsal that she wished she would have the sort of luck to find a Young Canadian pin! She said her grandfather collects all sorts of Stampede memorabilia. She's always looking for stuff for him."

"Did you look at Clay's pin?" asked Jessie.

Daisy was surprised. "You don't think...?"

"Are you *sure* it's not yours?" Jessie asked.

"I don't think Clay would take my pin. If he did, why would he wear it in front of me?" Daisy shook her head. "My aunt's pin has her name engraved on it so I'll know it when I find it."

"Did you actually see Clay's pin?" Violet asked.

Daisy paused. "No," she said finally. "I didn't see the pin close up." She changed the subject "Do you want to watch our rehearsal this afternoon? I'd like to know you're watching. That might be good luck!"

"I'd like to watch," Benny said.

Meanwhile Jessie was wondering about Marian. She had seemed so embarrassed the evening before when she and Henry had found her in the dressing room. She wondered why had Marian been hiding in the closet. Daisy didn't want to blame anyone, but Jessie had a feeling that someone had taken the pin.

They finished their smokies and made their way toward the grandstand. At this time of day, the stage was to the side of the rodeo arena and quiet.

As they came closer, the backstage door opened, and a woman dressed in cleaning coveralls stepped out and placed a beat-up box at the foot of the steps. Then she went back in and brought out a smaller box. Both were overflowing with old costumes and other stuff.

"Is that garbage?" Jessie asked.

"That's one of the cleaning crew," Daisy answered. "They were supposed to get rid of that old stuff from last year before our performances started this summer."

A few moments later, Marian came out from the same door. She hopped down the steps to see what was in the boxes and started to pull out something. But then she saw Daisy and the Aldens approaching, and she stood up as they passed. She even held open the door for them.

Jessie had the feeling Marian didn't want them to see what she was doing.

"Can I watch the part of the rehearsal with the wagon wheels now?" asked Benny as the door closed behind them.

Daisy pulled out her schedule. "Clay is one of the boys working with the wheels, Benny," she said. "They're practicing next. Why don't you come with me?" She and Benny went to watch.

"Let's go back outside," whispered Jessie to Henry and Violet.

Henry opened the door a crack, and they peered through and watched as Marian pulled clothing out of the first box and papers out of the second. She left the big box and put the stuff she'd collected into the smaller one and walked away in the direction of the river.

The Aldens waited a moment.

"Is it safe to follow her?" asked Violet.

"I think so," said Henry. "But don't let the door slam."

They eased out and closed the door carefully. If Marian looked back she would have seen them, but she didn't. She continued to walk toward the river while the Aldens followed, sometimes taking cover behind trees or bushes.

When Marian reached the river, the Aldens could see her approach Mr. Sutton, who was sitting on one of the large rocks by the river, his cowboy hat on his head as always. Marian sat next to her grandfather, and together they looked through the box.

The Aldens could hear the old man exclaim something. Even with his thick beard, they could see that he was smiling, and he clapped his hands together. He held up one of the old costumes, and put it into the bag he kept over his shoulder. Marian dug her hand into her pocket and pulled out something that fit in her hand. She held it out to him, and he took a look at it, put it in his own pocket,

and clapped his hands again. He emptied the remaining contents of the box into his bag and put it back over his shoulder. He looked very pleased.

Marian carried the empty box back to the stage door while the Aldens stayed hidden behind a tree. She didn't spot them as she passed and went back inside the grandstand.

Meanwhile, Mr. Sutton got to his feet and headed in the direction of the fairgrounds gates.

"Should we follow him?" Henry asked.

"I don't know how we'll get a chance to look in that bag," said Jessie. "It's always on his shoulder. We should probably talk to Marian instead."

When the Aldens let themselves back in through the stage door, Marian was busily organizing props and costume pieces on a table, preparing for the evening performance.

"We saw you with your grandfather just now," Jessie began. "It looked like you were giving him an old costume."

Marian frowned. "The cleaning people were just getting rid of some old stuff, and the stage manager told me I could look through it. She knows my Poppa is a collector. That's all you saw." Her eyes narrowed. "You still think I took the pin, don't you? What about that pin of Clay's? He *says* he bought it weeks ago. But don't you think it's funny that he started wearing it just after Daisy's went missing? How do you know he didn't sand Judy Simon's name off the back and make up the story about a yard sale?" She stared back at the Aldens, and her face grew redder and redder, but she didn't take her eyes away until they all heard a voice behind them.

"Violet? Henry? Jessie?" Grandfather had just come in the stage door. "I've come to pick you up for dinner," he said just as Daisy and Benny returned from watching rehearsal.

"We'll leave Daisy and the Young Canadians to prepare for their show," Grandfather said, smiling at Daisy. "I'm looking forward to it."

Daisy tried to smile back, but her smile seemed wobbly, Jessie thought, and she blinked as if she might cry.

As the Aldens prepared to leave with

Grandfather, Jessie turned to look back at Marian, whose face was still red.

"It was just some bits and pieces and an old costume," she said softly to Jessie. "Nothing anyone else but my poppa wants."

Jessie wished she could be sure of that.

CHAPTER 7

A Mystery Guest

"I'd still like to know what Mr. Sutton put in that bag of his," Henry said, as they waited in line for one of the many restaurants on Stephens Avenue Walk. Benny had picked a hamburger place when he'd seen the menu posted by the front door. "They put cheese and apples on one of their burgers!"

While the Aldens waited to be seated, they talked about the mystery.

"I'd like to see the pin that Clay has. Do you think it would look different if it had been engraved and the engraving was removed?" asked Jessie.

"I'd like to see what Marian had in her hand when she handed something small to her poppa," said Violet.

"I'd like to have Aunt Judy with us so we don't have to wait in line," said Benny.

The others laughed. "You really think Aunt Judy never has to wait for anything?" asked Henry.

"Yes," said Benny.

"Where is Aunt Judy?" asked Violet.

"I don't know," Grandfather said. "She just sent a message saying she'd meet up with us later."

"Boy, I hope she doesn't go missing too," said Benny.

"I'm sure she'll show up in time for the Grandstand Show," Grandfather said.

The restaurant host seated the Aldens at a table on the patio, circled by a low wall made up of bales of hay. Benny was excited to see more wagon wheels leaning against the hay. Jessie pointed out the Western skirts that some girls walking down the sidewalk were wearing. Henry admired the cowboy belts other pedestrians wore. He wouldn't mind a fancy belt buckle for himself.

"Do people always dress like this here?" he asked. "Or is it special, just for the Stampede?"

A man at the next table overheard his question and gave a chuckle. "Boy," he called, "we like our cowboy hats here all year long."

After dinner, the Aldens returned to the Grandstand, where they took their seats. There was no sign of Aunt Judy, though Violet was sure the empty seat beside them was hers. She tried not to feel worried.

"We didn't get to sit out here last night!" said Henry. "It's going to be different watching the show from out here in the stands."

"The show doesn't start for another hour. What's happening now?" asked Jessie.

A woman sitting just in front of them turned to answer. "Every evening at this time is the chuck wagon races. The chuck wagons are my favorite part of the whole Stampede! You'll see!"

The rodeo arena was filling with brightly painted covered wagons, each hitched with four lively horses. One wagon had flames painted on the sides, and another was yellow with bold orange polka-dots. Violet cheered for the one painted like a rainbow.

"How do they race in the arena?" asked Henry. "It's too small."

"It is," said the helpful spectator. She pointed out how the chuck wagon course went outside of the rodeo arena and around a huge track that surrounded both the arena and far seating. "We can watch all the action on that!" She pointed to a huge screen set up at one end of the rodeo arena. "The wagons will circle back into the arena right in front of us, coming down the straightaway to the finish line."

"Wow!" Henry said.

Four large white barrels were placed across the arena to mark starting places for each of the wagons. As the contestants and their horses readied for the race, the Aldens could feel excitement all around them. Many spectators went to stand at the railing for a closer view of the track.

The horses had been moving slowly,

pulling wagons into place, shaking their beautiful necks, whinnying, but when the horn sounded, suddenly they leapt into a run in a burst of powerful energy.

"They've been waiting for this!" said Jessie. "Look at them go!"

"Let's get a better view too!" shouted Grandfather over the noise. The Aldens hurried down the grandstand aisle toward the railing.

The horses pulled the wagons hard, circling the barrels and sweeping up and around the huge oval track. The overhead screen showed the wagon teams racing behind the stands, and the Aldens readied themselves for the final straightaway in front of them.

The cheering became even louder as the horses reached the straightaway and came barreling down. Jessie knew she was hollering but she couldn't even hear herself. Henry was laughing at her and shouting something too, and Violet and Benny were holding on to her sleeves as if to keep her from flying away with excitement.

All the wagon drivers were standing, urging their horses to go faster and faster. The driver of the lead wagon yelled the loudest and his hat went flying. The ground shook as the horses and wagons sped past. The wind tangled the girls' long hair over their faces. Violet pushed hers out of her eyes, and Jessie twisted hers back into a knot.

"I think some horse snot flew out and landed on me," yelled Benny.

A new group of four horse-and-wagon teams prepared for the next race, and Grandfather led the way back to their seats. Violet kept looking over her shoulder. She didn't want to miss a second of it, even though it scared her a bit too.

After six more groups of wagons and horses, more thundering and shaking ground, and more cheering and excitement, the chuck wagon races were over for that evening.

Everyone watched as the stage was pulled into the rodeo arena by an enormous tractor. Soon the arena was ready for the evening Grandstand Show. Then, with a blast of music and lights, the Young Canadians took the stage.

"There's Clay with that wagon wheel!" Benny said. He was perched on the edge of his seat as Clay whirled his wagon wheel into the air and caught it again and again.

Suddenly Clay fumbled and dropped his wheel, but he caught it so quickly that only someone watching closely would have seen it. "Did you see that?" Benny's voice was shrill. "He got it. He saved the day. He didn't really drop it."

"Now *that* takes a lot of practice," said Grandfather.

Next up was Daisy. This time she didn't attempt to sing by herself. She brought Clay and the girl who had helped her the night before, and once again they sang as a trio. They sounded so good that the audience clapped a long time when they finished.

Then the show's announcer told the audience to welcome a mystery guest. "Every Calgary Grandstand Show has one," he said. "And this one is extra special." As he spoke, a bright silver bus drove up a ramp onto the stage.

The Aldens leaned forward to get a closer

look at the bus just as a man was making his way past their seats and blocking their view for a moment. It was Mr. Sutton.

"Hello," he said. He was about to sit in the seat meant for Aunt Judy, but first he picked up something that someone had left underneath the seat. It was a ticket stub. "Here's a find!" he said and tucked it into his leather bag. Then he sat down.

"You're not Aunt Judy," said Benny.

"No, I'm not," replied Mr. Sutton. "*There's* Aunt Judy," he said, pointing to the stage.

The entire side of the bus opened up almost magically, and inside was another stage, complete with flashing red and gold lights.

And there was Aunt Judy, wearing a glittering dress and a microphone in hand.

"Hello, Calgary!" she shouted, and the crowd roared their approval. "It's so good to be home!" She sang about coming home from a long time traveling. Her voice was rich and mellow.

Violet looked over at Grandfather. "You're right," she said. "She is a great singer. Even better than she sounds in her kitchen singing about cows and soup."

Grandfather smiled. "I remember when she first sang this song," he said. "She wrote it when she was traveling and homesick. It's my favorite."

"She's our best," said Mr. Sutton proudly. "I have a photograph of her the first time she was onstage."

Henry looked at Mr. Sutton and wondered again what else he might have—*the pin*?

Aunt Judy sang more songs. The entire audience sang along with one of them.

"Everyone knows all words!" said Violet. "They must really love her music."

"Before I start my last song," Aunt Judy said, "I'd like to ask my niece to join me!" The crowd cheered. "This is a song we've sung together since she was a very small girl!"

Daisy waved to the crowd from the back of the stage. The crowd cheered in response. Aunt Judy motioned to Daisy to join her on the bus, and the crowd cheered even louder. But when Daisy reached Aunt Judy, the Aldens could see Daisy shake her head. Aunt Judy whispered to her, and Daisy stopped shaking her head. Aunt Judy gave her a hug and began the song.

Daisy came in on the harmony with just a soft voice at first, then louder and louder when her aunt let her take over for an entire verse. Aunt Judy stepped back from Daisy and moved away to stand with the back-up singers.

"Look at that!" said Jessie. "Daisy is singing on her own now!"

The crowd was thrilled. Two Young Canadians, one from the past and one from the present, were up onstage together. They audience stood and clapped when Daisy finished. Aunt Judy stepped forward and clapped for her niece too.

Jessie turned to Henry. "Daisy really doesn't need that pin, does she?" she said. Henry grinned. Violet and Benny shook their heads.

"No, she doesn't," said Benny. "She can be brave all on her own."

The side of Aunt Judy's special bus folded up and closed. It drove back down the ramp and out of the stampede arena.

The fireworks show followed the musical program, and Violet and Benny both said it was even better than the previous night. "It wasn't this long," said Jessie, remembering how she and Henry had felt very short on time looking for the pin in the dressing room.

"There's more purple tonight!" said Violet happily, looking skyward to the colorful explosions.

The show ended with a series of deep booms that echoed across the fairgrounds. The children stood to go.

"We still need to find the pin," said Henry, "even if Daisy doesn't need it to perform."

Jessie turned to Mr. Sutton, who was looking through his bag.

"Mr. Sutton," she began, "Marian gave you a costume."

"That's right," he said. He didn't even ask how she knew. "She finds some wonderful pieces for my collection. Whatever I don't add to the collection, I give to our little neighbor."

"Your little neighbor?" Jessie asked.

"I think you've met her," he said. "Clay's little sister."

"You're neighbors?" Henry asked.

"Yes, she and Clay live just a few doors

away. She loves costumes."

"What about other collectible pieces? The other day, we saw Marian give you something small. Was it a Young Canadian pin, by any chance?" asked Jessie.

Mr. Sutton gave her a sharp look. "Marian said you're looking for that missing pin and seem to think she had something to do with it. I can assure you, she doesn't. I do think that pin should be in the museum, but *I* wouldn't take it."

He put his bag over his shoulder and got up to leave.

They watched him go.

"I don't think he liked being questioned like that," Henry said.

"What should we do now?" Jessie asked.

"I don't know what to do about the mystery," said Henry, "but we should really find Aunt Judy and Daisy and tell them how much we enjoyed their show!"

Chapter 8

A Good Catch

Back in the dressing room, the mood was festive. Everyone seemed pleased to have Aunt Judy sing in the show. Young Canadians gathered around her to hear stories of her time in their shoes. Daisy's cheeks were pink and her eyes were shiny.

Henry noticed that Clay had changed into a T-shirt and shorts. He was sitting at the makeup counter, though the bright lights around the mirrors were off, and it was a bit dark on that side of the room. The counter was covered with bouquets of roses and other flowers sent to congratulate the performers. Marian was nearby putting the bouquets in vases.

Clay seemed to be the only person in the room who was not happy.

"I think that's because he dropped the wagon wheel," whispered Benny. "I'm going to cheer him up." He and Henry approached Clay.

"I like how you caught that wheel before anyone noticed," Benny said.

"*You* noticed," Clay said glumly.

"But you caught it so quickly. My grandfather says that takes lots of practice," Benny replied.

"Your grandfather says it takes lots of practice to *drop* a wheel?" Clay asked.

"No, it takes lots of practice to make a mistake and fix it before anyone can notice," Henry said.

Henry noticed that Marian, who had been listening nearby, looked startled when he said that. For a moment she even looked at Henry.

"Is something wrong?" Henry asked her.

"Nothing," she said quickly. She grabbed a broom leaning against the wall and began to sweep the floor. She kept her face down and didn't look at them again.

Clay picked up his performing shirt from where he'd tossed it on the counter. He fingered the pin on his shirt and looked dismayed. "I really thought this pin would bring me good luck," he said.

"Good luck doesn't come from a thing like that," said Daisy, overhearing the conversation. It comes from all our hard work. I think my aunt was right after all."

Clay undid the pin and looked at it closely as if it could tell him a secret. At last he placed it on the counter and got up and left the room.

Henry picked up the pin for a closer look. He turned it over to see if it might have been engraved. He didn't see anything suspicious, but the pin did feel a bit scratched under his fingertips.

His sisters came closer and Benny hovered at his elbows eager for a look.

"What do you think?" Henry asked.

Each of them took a turn inspecting the pin.

Violet pointed to some marks on the back. "It looks as if someone dropped it on the sidewalk and stepped on it," she said.

"Or could it have been engraved and then scratched off?" Jessie held the pin up to her eyes and turned toward the light in the room.

"Quick," said Benny, hearing the bathroom door open and close down the hall. "I think Clay's coming back."

But it was Little Clay who entered the dressing room with her shy smile. "What are you doing?" she asked.

Just then Jessie had an idea. "Little Clay, do you know how long Clay has had this pin?" she asked.

"Weeks and weeks and weeks and weeks," Little Clay answered.

"Are you sure?" asked Henry. That would mean the pin couldn't possibly be Daisy's.

"Of course I'm sure," Little Clay said. "I gave it back to him, because he needs some luck. Did you see him drop that wagon wheel?"

Clay was suddenly behind her. "What are you saying?" he asked in a really grouchy voice.

"I'm just talking about that wagon wheel..." his little sister started to say.

"See?" said Clay, turning to Benny. "It wasn't just you who saw it. Everyone saw my mistake. Even my little sister."

Little Clay looked dismayed at first, but slowly a smile grew on her face. She leaned toward her brother and whispered something in his ear.

His face went from grumpy to a half smile. Then it stretched to a full smile. He gave a chuckle. "I'd forgotten how you make me laugh sometimes," he told Little Clay.

"You have been pretty grouchy lately," she said, not whispering anymore.

"I'm sorry," he said. It sounded as if he really meant it.

"I get it," said Little Clay. "I know what it's like to be scared to get up in front of people and sing and dance."

"I think you should have the pin!" said Big Clay.

"No," said Little Clay. "I don't need it. I already have—"

Crash!

Marian had been sweeping the broom around Clay and his little sister and under the makeup counter. Now she'd accidentally bumped one of the vases of flowers off the counter and it had come tumbling down. Water and flowers and pieces of the ceramic vase were all over the floor. "Oh no!" she cried.

The other performers rushed in to help, and Jessie gave Marian a hug.

"It's only an old vase," one of the performers said. "Nothing to be bothered about." The floor was clean in minutes.

Before long all the Young Canadians were out of costume and ready to go home. They drifted out in groups, and soon just the Aldens, Daisy, Clay, and Little Clay were left.

"So what did Little Clay whisper to you?" Jessie asked Clay.

"She told me I shouldn't worry about dropping the wheel, because everyone knows what I was doing is *wheely wheely* hard to do!" He laughed. "It made me realize I was silly to be so worried about anyone noticing me drop the wheel. Benny was right: my catch was a good one."

Benny agreed. "It was a good catch!"

Chapter 9

Skyride

The Aldens arrived at the gate to Stampede Park first thing the next morning. "I'd really like to go on the Skyride before we go home," said Violet.

"We have a mystery to solve," Jessie reminded her.

"But we need a break!" said Benny. "We can have a break and ride the Skyride."

Stampede Park had a sleepy feel to it that morning as if the excitement of the first two days was over. "It's almost like having the place to ourselves," said Henry.

"Maybe we should take a break," Jessie said, and she pointed to the ride. "Look at the line for the Skyride!"

"What line?" asked Benny.

"Exactly!" said Jessie.

Only three people were waiting for the ride, and the Aldens took their places behind them.

Soon they were up in the sky, Violet and Henry sitting together, and Jessie and Benny in the gondola behind them. Violet loved the feeling as they swept up into the air—like taking off in an airplane. The ride paused for a moment, and the seats bobbed up and down a bit. She didn't feel too good about that, but then the ride started up again and went gliding over the fairgrounds.

Henry smiled at Violet. "All right?" he asked.

Violet gave a little wiggle of happiness. "Yes!"

Below them was a mosaic of colors. They could hear laughter and chatting, music and singing, and animals bleating and mooing. Smells of popcorn and hotdogs wafted their way.

"Hey!" called Jessie.

Violet had almost forgotten that Jessie and Benny were in the gondola behind. She turned to see her sister pointing down at someone.

Mr. Sutton was behind a building going through a garbage dumpster.

Violet twisted in her seat to watch him as the Skyride moved along.

Jessie and Benny were watching too.

"What do you think he's doing?" Henry asked.

"I don't know," Violet said.

They watched until Mr. Sutton was out of sight.

"The ride is almost over," said Henry. "We'll try to find him."

Everything looked a bit different once they were on the ground, but the Aldens set off quickly and managed to find the building they'd spotted on the ride. As they rounded the corner, Mr. Sutton was just disappearing around another corner, his shoulder bag looking heavy. He had another full bag in his hand.

"Follow him!" said Henry.

The Aldens followed Mr. Sutton through the crowds of fairgoers. The grounds had been almost empty when they arrived, but now the fair was filling up, so they had a hard time keeping their eyes on him. He was heading toward the Saddledome, the huge stadium shaped like a saddle. It was in a corner of Stampede Park that the Aldens had not yet explored.

Jessie chuckled and took his hand. "It's a good thing our Mr. Sutton has on a dinosaur-sized cowboy hat, otherwise we'd never be able to follow him like this!

Mr. Sutton took a quick left through another long barn, and then another quick turn left between horse stalls. They children almost lost him, but Violet spotted him and called out, "Over there!"

Then they were all in front of the Saddledome with its red entranceway.

"*Now* what is Mr. Sutton doing?" said Jessie.

Mr. Sutton didn't go into the building. He walked farther along and paused near a concrete column covered with posters. The Aldens moved closer and watched.

He was taking down a poster from the column. Then he took another. The children circled him.

"Mr. Sutton?" said Henry.

The old man started, but when he saw Henry, he smiled. "Isn't this a nice one?" he said and held out the poster for the children to see. "Someone missed this poster," he said, and Jessie looked closely at the thick, colorful paper to see what he meant. He pointed to the date on it. The date was from the previous summer. "Here, you hold it while I put this one back."

She held the poster while he replaced the newer poster.

"This one," he explained, pointing to the one he'd just put up again, "was covering that one. A poster left over from last summer is a treasure!" he said, his eyes shiny. He took it from Jessie and carefully rolled it up and slipped it inside a cardboard roll from his shoulder bag.

"What's in your bag?" Benny asked Mr. Sutton. "Is it full of treasures?"

Mr. Sutton smiled. “Yes, it is.”

“Where do you keep all the treasures you find?” asked Henry.

“Somewhere we could see?” asked Jessie.

The old man looked at them. “You want to see my collection?”

The Aldens looked at each other. “We’d like that very much,” said Jessie. “Let’s find Aunt Judy, and she can take us. You can show us the way.”

“All right,” said Mr. Sutton. He sounded pleased.

They found Aunt Judy having lunch with Daisy at a picnic table by the river. They’d bought sandwiches for all of them and offered an extra one to Mr. Sutton too. They collected the sandwiches and headed toward Aunt Judy’s van.

Mr. Sutton directed her onto the highway leading to the far corner of town.

“I’m so pleased that all of you want to see my collection,” he said. “I love showing it. So many people just don’t care about artifacts.”

“We’re happy to see it,” said Aunt Judy.

“Wow! This sandwich is weird, but good,”

said Benny from the back seat. "What is it?"

Aunt Judy laughed. "Deep fried jalapeno tofu on a bun, Benny," she said. "I told you: it's a competition here at the Stampede to see who can come up with the strangest food. That can mean deep-fried anything!"

Benny had to think about that for a moment. "Wow!"

Mr. Sutton directed Aunt Judy to pull into a driveway. "Here is my home," he said. "Marian and her mother live upstairs and I live downstairs. I have a small barn out back." He took them around to the back of the house to a little barn-shaped house.

He unlocked the door, and the Aldens were surprised to see a miniature museum inside. *Cow Town Amateur Archives!* said a sign hanging from the ceiling.

"These Stampede posters are just like the ones at the Glenbow Museum," said Benny. "But some have water stains," he added, looking closer.

"My little group of Cow Town Amateur Archivists rescued those from the flood," Mr. Sutton said.

In the middle of the room were glass counters with shelves inside filled with coins, postcards, passes for midway rides, and all sorts of Stampede mementos.

"Oh, look!" said Violet, pointing to a large unfolded fan with a bucking bronco painted on it.

"This is amazing!" said Jessie, and Mr. Sutton smiled. Daisy was carefully looking through each item under the glass.

"Where does all this come from?" asked Aunt Judy.

"I've collected these treasures since I was a little boy going to the Stampede. I started the first year my father took me to the Stampede. My family didn't have much money. My father would buy just the tickets to get in, and we couldn't buy the special program with the descriptions of all the rodeo events and photos of the cowboys. I really wanted one of those. One day—I'll never forget it—I found a program that someone had just abandoned on his seat. He hadn't even bothered to throw it away in the trash. After that, I found all sorts of things. People don't take care of treasures."

"But you do," said Violet. "And now all these treasures are here."

"That's right," Mr. Sutton said.

"Oh!" said Aunt Judy from a corner. "Will you look at this!"

The children gathered around her. She was looking at a poster of herself on the far wall. Below the poster were some shelves with ticket stubs to her concerts, a funny old Stampede mug with her face on it, and an official Grandstand Show photo of Aunt Judy as a teenager.

On a nearby mannequin was a red-and-white child-size dress with a huge maple leaf in the middle of the skirt. Aunt Judy smiled. "That looks like a costume I wore years ago to celebrate Canada Day! Wherever did you find that?"

"Someone came across a box of costumes that were almost ruined by the flood," replied Mr. Sutton. "She gave the box to me because she knows about my collection and the work of the Amateur Archives. I have a few friends who help me with this work."

"We remember your float in the parade,"

said Henry, and the rest of Aldens nodded in agreement.

"All these artifacts," Jessie said slowly, "are things that need you to care for them."

Mr. Sutton nodded. "Look at this!" he said, reaching into his pocket for something. Jessie had a feeling he was about to show the item his granddaughter had handed him on the riverbank the day before.

It was an ancient bottle cap from a bottle of Crush soda. "Marian found it to add to my collection," he said gleefully. He motioned to another display, this one of bottle caps in all colors. Some looked very old.

Henry turned to his siblings. "I don't think we're going to find Daisy's pin here."

Mr. Sutton shook his head. "I never take things that don't belong to me."

Aunt Judy spoke up. "We know that. Mr. Sutton, thank you for showing us your collection."

"Thank you," he said. "I like when other people enjoy our collection."

"But we still haven't found my pin," said Daisy.

Henry looked at his siblings. "Well," he

said, “if it’s not here, and Marian doesn’t have it…then there’s only one other person who would.”

Jessie spoke up. “And she likes costumes and anything to do with Young Canadians. Or being a Young Canadian.”

“I think we need to go visit down the street,” said Henry.

CHAPTER 10

The Other Greatest Outdoor Show On Earth

Mr. Sutton fetched Marian before the group set off down the street.

As they neared Clay's house, they could hear music coming from the backyard. Daisy recognized it as a recording of one of the songs the Young Canadians performed. There was the sound of applause and cheering.

When the group rounded the corner of the house they found a low deck on the back of the house decorated to look like a stage. Somebody had painted props, including a

YC

barn and big, green chickens. Dried cornstalks lined the edge of the stage. A group of kids from the neighborhood were sitting on bales of hay in the yard below the stage.

Little Clay was taking bows onstage. The show was just finished, and some of the neighbor children drifted back to their own yards while a few of them stayed to play in a sandbox in the corner of the yard.

Little Clay saw the Aldens and their friends approach and climbed down the porch steps to meet them.

"Oh my," said Aunt Judy when she caught sight of the pin on Little Clay's shirt collar. "You have the pin."

Little Clay looked at Aunt Judy and then at the rest of the group. She touched the pin. "Are you looking for this?" she asked. "I started to wonder about it. You were making such a big deal about Clay's pin."

Clay came out of the house just then and made his way over to the group. "What…?" he started to say as he saw his little sister undo the pin on her shirt.

She looked at the pin in her hands. "I found

it on the floor," mumbled Little Clay. Her voice was so soft they could hardly hear her. "I thought no one wanted it."

"But it was in my locker," said Daisy. She tried to keep her voice gentle but she felt frustrated. She was surprised Little Clay didn't know not to take things that didn't belong to her. Then Marian spoke up, and her voice was a whisper. "Little Clay is telling the truth," she said. "It was on the floor. I know... because I was the one who dropped it."

Daisy gasped. "Dropped it?"

Marian sounded miserable. "I was the one who picked it up when I saw your locker door open, Daisy. It was sitting there, and I...I just wanted to see it."

Everyone stared at her, and she turned very red, reminding Henry of the first time he'd ever seen her.

"It's like you said about making a mistake and trying to fix it," she said. "I admit it crossed my mind to take it. But I thought I couldn't do that because it wouldn't be right. I started to put it back in your locker, Daisy. Then somebody came rushing through the room, ran by me, and knocked it right out of my hand. I searched everywhere, but I couldn't find it!"

Clay looked at her. "I think that was me," he said. "I was rushing around in a panic looking for my missing cowboy hat."

Little Clay spoke up. "I saw the pin under the counter in the dressing room. It looked like it was forgotten. I thought having my own pin would make me into a Young Canadian too. It was just like Big Clay's so I could return his."

Clay spoke up and he sounded grumpy. "Can you just call me Clay?" he said. "I'm so tired of being 'Big Clay.'"

Little Clay paused. "Okay. But you'll have to call me Melody."

"Melody?" asked Jessie.

"That's my real name." Melody stood straighter. "I'm going to be Melody from now on."

"I think Melody's a perfect name for a singer," said Violet.

Melody looked at all of them. "I'm sorry," she said. "I should have known somebody would be looking for this pin."

"Give it to Daisy," said Clay. "It's hers."

Melody handed it to Daisy, and Daisy pinned it to her own collar. Shyly Melody said, "It looks really nice on you."

"Thank you," said Daisy. "I'm glad to have it back. I'm even more glad to know that I don't really need it—not like I thought I did. In fact, maybe I should think about giving it to the museum, like Mr. Sutton keeps saying." She looked at Aunt Judy. "Would you be all right with that?"

Aunt Judy nodded. "I'm so happy you know you don't really need it."

Clay spoke up. "I think you should keep it, not for good luck, but because it was your aunt's, and she's a special person in your life." He dug around in his pocket for his pin. "I found this at a yard sale. That makes it a great find, but not something really special for me. I think this one should go to the museum. What do you think, Melody?" he asked his little sister.

"That's a good place for it," she said.

"Hey!" said Aunt Judy. "Why don't you and I and Daisy all sing a song together?"

Melody looked shy again for a moment. "I only like to sing for my friends," she said.

"Then think of us as friends," said Jessie.

"Because we *are* your friends," Violet added. It was true. She knew that she, Jessie, Henry, and Benny would never forget everyone they had met on this trip. They were so glad they'd come to Calgary.

Daisy reached for Melody's hand, and they went up onto the deck. "Do you know the song about the cow in my soup?"

"That's my favorite," said Melody.

"Mine too," said Aunt Judy. "I think the Aldens can sing with us."

"And Mr. Sutton and Marian?"

"Everybody. You start us off, Daisy."

And she did, loud and clear.

BASED ON THE **WORLDWIDE BEST-SELLER**

Create everyday adventures with the Boxcar Children Guide to Adventure!

A fun compendium filled with tips and tricks from the Boxcar Children—from making invisible ink and secret disguises, creating secret codes, and packing a suitcase to taking the perfect photo and enjoying the great outdoors.

Available wherever books are sold

The adventures continue in the newest mysteries!

PB ISBN: 9780807508961, $5.99

PB ISBN: 9780807556061, $5.99

THE BOXCAR CHILDREN

THE MYSTERY OF THE STOLEN DINOSAUR BONES

Created by
GERTRUDE CHANDLER WARNER

PB ISBN: 9780807556085, $5.99

Read on for an exclusive sneak peek of the newest Boxcar Children Mystery!

PB ISBN: 9780807528440, $5.99

Before they could ring the bell, a figure carrying a lantern came out of the shadows between the buildings. Violet, who was in front, let out a little squeak of surprise and took a step back.

"Don't be frightened," a woman's voice called. As she came forward, the lantern light showed a woman about Mrs. McGregor's age.

"Gretchen!" Mrs. McGregor exclaimed. "We were worried when we didn't see any lights. Children, this is my dear friend Mrs. Vanderhoff."

Mrs. Vanderhoff said, "I'm delighted to meet you. Now let me guess who is who. I've heard so much about you."

"Guess me first! Please!" Benny raised his hand.

"Hmmm...well, I know Henry is fourteen years old. Are you Henry?" She smiled when she said this to Benny and the older children knew she was teasing.

"No." Benny laughed. "I'm only six."

"Then you must be Benny, and the taller boy must be Henry."

"You're right!" Benny said. "Can you guess the girls?"

Mrs. Vanderhoff smiled again. "The girls are easier to guess because I've heard Violet likes purple and I see one of you has on a purple sweater."

Violet nodded.

"I also know you're an artist," Mrs. Vanderhoff continued. "I hope you brought your paints! The Hudson River Valley is a famous spot for painting."

"I did bring them," Violet said. "I would like to try to paint some of the trees with their fall colors."

Mrs. Vanderhoff turned to Violet's sister. "So you must be Jessie," she said, shaking Jessie's hand. "And I'd recognize Watch anywhere." She patted the dog, and the terrier wagged his tail. "I'm sorry it's so dark, but the power is out," she explained.

"The dark made your porch look scary," Benny said.

"We thought the scarecrow was a headless man," Violet added.

Mrs. Vanderhoff looked puzzled. "The scarecrow isn't supposed to be scary. My daughter Annika carved a happy face on the pumpkin head."

"The pumpkin head is on the ground," Jessie said. Henry shone the flashlight so Mrs. Vanderhoff could see it.

"Oh, that's too bad. The pumpkin must have fallen off the scarecrow frame. Annika wouldn't make a headless scarecrow. She doesn't like scary Halloween decorations. We'll fix the scarecrow tomorrow."

Gertrude Chandler Warner discovered when she was teaching that many readers who like an exciting story could find no books that were both easy and fun to read. She decided to try to meet this need, and her first book, *The Boxcar Children*, quickly proved she had succeeded.

Miss Warner drew on her own experiences to write the mystery. As a child she spent hours watching trains go by on the tracks opposite her family home. She often dreamed about what it would be like to set up housekeeping in a caboose or freight car—the situation the Alden children find themselves in.

While the mystery element is central to each of Miss Warner's books, she never thought of them as strictly juvenile mysteries. She liked to stress the Aldens' independence and resourcefulness and their solid New England devotion to using up and making do. The Aldens go about most of their adventures with as little adult supervision as possible—something else that delights young readers.

Miss Warner lived in Putnam, Connecticut, until her death in 1979. During her lifetime, she received hundreds of letters from girls and boys telling her how much they liked her books.

The Boxcar Children Mysteries

The Boxcar Children
Surprise Island
The Yellow House Mystery
Mystery Ranch
Mike's Mystery
Blue Bay Mystery
The Woodshed Mystery
The Lighthouse Mystery
Mountain Top Mystery
Schoolhouse Mystery
Caboose Mystery
Houseboat Mystery
Snowbound Mystery
Tree House Mystery
Bicycle Mystery
Mystery in the Sand
Mystery Behind the Wall
Bus Station Mystery
Benny Uncovers a Mystery
The Haunted Cabin Mystery
The Deserted Library Mystery
The Animal Shelter Mystery
The Old Motel Mystery
The Mystery of the Hidden Painting
The Amusement Park Mystery
The Mystery of the Mixed-Up Zoo
The Camp-Out Mystery
The Mystery Girl
The Mystery Cruise
The Disappearing Friend Mystery
The Mystery of the Singing Ghost
The Mystery in the Snow
The Pizza Mystery
The Mystery Horse
The Mystery at the Dog Show
The Castle Mystery
The Mystery of the Lost Village
The Mystery on the Ice
The Mystery of the Purple Pool
The Ghost Ship Mystery
The Mystery in Washington, DC
The Canoe Trip Mystery
The Mystery of the Hidden Beach
The Mystery of the Missing Cat
The Mystery at Snowflake Inn
The Mystery on Stage
The Dinosaur Mystery
The Mystery of the Stolen Music
The Mystery at the Ball Park
The Chocolate Sundae Mystery
The Mystery of the Hot Air Balloon
The Mystery Bookstore
The Pilgrim Village Mystery
The Mystery of the Stolen Boxcar
The Mystery in the Cave
The Mystery on the Train
The Mystery at the Fair
The Mystery of the Lost Mine
The Guide Dog Mystery
The Hurricane Mystery
The Pet Shop Mystery
The Mystery of the Secret Message
The Firehouse Mystery
The Mystery in San Francisco
The Niagara Falls Mystery
The Mystery at the Alamo
The Outer Space Mystery
The Soccer Mystery
The Mystery in the Old Attic
The Growling Bear Mystery
The Mystery of the Lake Monster
The Mystery at Peacock Hall
The Windy City Mystery
The Black Pearl Mystery
The Cereal Box Mystery
The Panther Mystery
The Mystery of the Queen's Jewels
The Stolen Sword Mystery
The Basketball Mystery
The Movie Star Mystery
The Mystery of the Pirate's Map
The Ghost Town Mystery
The Mystery of the Black Raven
The Mystery in the Mall

The Boxcar Children Mysteries

The Mystery in New York
The Gymnastics Mystery
The Poison Frog Mystery
The Mystery of the Empty Safe
The Home Run Mystery
The Great Bicycle Race Mystery
The Mystery of the Wild Ponies
The Mystery in the Computer Game
The Honeybee Mystery
The Mystery at the Crooked House
The Hockey Mystery
The Mystery of the Midnight Dog
The Mystery of the Screech Owl
The Summer Camp Mystery
The Copycat Mystery
The Haunted Clock Tower Mystery
The Mystery of the Tiger's Eye
The Disappearing Staircase Mystery
The Mystery on Blizzard Mountain
The Mystery of the Spider's Clue
The Candy Factory Mystery
The Mystery of the Mummy's Curse
The Mystery of the Star Ruby
The Stuffed Bear Mystery
The Mystery of Alligator Swamp
The Mystery at Skeleton Point
The Tattletale Mystery
The Comic Book Mystery
The Great Shark Mystery
The Ice Cream Mystery
The Midnight Mystery
The Mystery in the Fortune Cookie
The Black Widow Spider Mystery
The Radio Mystery
The Mystery of the Runaway Ghost
The Finders Keepers Mystery
The Mystery of the Haunted Boxcar
The Clue in the Corn Maze
The Ghost of the Chattering Bones
The Sword of the Silver Knight
The Game Store Mystery
The Mystery of the Orphan Train
The Vanishing Passenger
The Giant Yo-Yo Mystery
The Creature in Ogopogo Lake
The Rock 'n' Roll Mystery
The Secret of the Mask
The Seattle Puzzle
The Ghost in the First Row
The Box That Watch Found
A Horse Named Dragon
The Great Detective Race
The Ghost at the Drive-In Movie
The Mystery of the Traveling Tomatoes
The Spy Game
The Dog-Gone Mystery
The Vampire Mystery
Superstar Watch
The Spy in the Bleachers
The Amazing Mystery Show
The Pumpkin Head Mystery
The Cupcake Caper
The Clue in the Recycling Bin
Monkey Trouble
The Zombie Project
The Great Turkey Heist
The Garden Thief
The Boardwalk Mystery
The Mystery of the Fallen Treasure
The Return of the Graveyard Ghost
The Mystery of the Stolen Snowboard
The Mystery of the Wild West Bandit
The Mystery of the Grinning Gargoyle
The Mystery of the Soccer Snitch
The Mystery of the Missing Pop Idol
The Mystery of the Stolen Dinosaur Bones
The Mystery at the Calgary Stampede
The Sleepy Hollow Mystery